Ruby and Grub

Abi Burlingham
Illustrated by Sarah Warburton

PICCADILLY PRESS • LONDON

This is me,
I'm Ruby.

This is Grub,
he's a grubby, mucky pup!

Grub loves to dig.

He digs and digs and digs.

When I shout,

"Stop digging!"

he doesn't stop digging.

Do you know what he does?

He carries on digging.

I don't think he can hear me.

Sometimes he turns on his side,
like this.
I say, "No, Grub, no!"
But he doesn't listen.

I say, "Walk, Grub, walk!"

Do you know what he does?

He rolls on his other side!

I think Grub's tired.

Sometimes,
Grub rolls over and over **SO** much
that he needs a bath.

I say, "In, Grub, in!"
Do you know what he does?
He leaps in the bath,
then he rolls over and over
IN THE BATH!

I say, "Oh no, Grub!"

Then I am wet too.

I look like **I'VE** had a bath!

I think Grub thinks it's funny.

It **is** quite funny.

Last week I had a bad tummy.
Grub sat by my bed
and wouldn't move –
ALL DAY!
"Bed, Grub!" I said.
Do you know what he did?
He sat on **MY** bed.
I think he thought it was **HIS** bed.

Then one day,
something **TERRIBLE** happened.
Grub got out!

Do you know what he did?
He chased the ice-cream van down the street
and the van had to stop.

I told him, "Grub, that's bad!
But then I thought,
"No, it's good,"
and I bought some ice-cream.

It was delicious!
Grub thought so too.

Then one day, something **EVEN MORE TERRIBLE** happened.

Grub dug a hole under our fence,

and under next door's fence.

It took six people to catch him and bring him back.

Mum wasn't pleased ONE BIT!
"**THAT IS IT!**" she said, "I've had enough!
Grub, you are just **TOO** naughty, **TOO** mucky
and **TOO** much trouble," she said.
"Grub, you will have to GO!"

I cried,
but Mum
wouldn't
budge.

So we took him to Uncle Tom's.
Uncle Tom had three dogs already.
He didn't mind one more.

When we got home,
it felt so strange without Grub
and I kept looking round, thinking,
"Where's Grub?"
Mum kept looking round, thinking,
"Where's Grub?"

Dad kept looking round, thinking,
"Where's Grub?"
Joe crawled round and round
the house until he was dizzy, shouting,
"**GUB! GUB!**"
The house didn't feel right
without Grub.

We stood in the garden.
It was a mess!
We filled in the holes that Grub dug.
It took ages!
Do you know what Joe did?
He started digging holes in the garden!
It didn't feel right without Grub.

I gave Sally a bath to make me feel better.

But she didn't splash about like Grub.

I splashed water on myself.

But it wasn't the same without Grub.

Mum bought us ice-creams to cheer us up.

But they didn't taste the same without Grub.

Mum said, "The garden's too tidy."

Dad said, "The house is too clean."

I said, "My bed feels lonely without Grub."

Joe screwed up his face until he looked as if he'd go **POP**
and screamed, "**GUB!!!**"

Nothing was the same
without Grub.

"**THAT IS IT!**" said Mum. "I've had enough!"

"Come on, let's go," said Dad.

So Mum and Dad and Joe and I all got in the car.

Do you know where we went?

We went to Uncle Tom's!

Grub raced out the house to see us.

Do you know what he did?

He ran around in circles.

He rolled in the mud.

He covered me in muddy paw prints.

"He's naughty, he's mucky
and he's far too much trouble," said Mum.
"But we just miss him TOO much."

"Please can he come home?" I asked Uncle Tom.
Uncle Tom didn't mind one bit.
He has three dogs already.

Now the house is a mess, the garden is a mess,

everywhere's a mess.

But it doesn't matter because . . .

I have Grub,
and Grub has me!